The Long Way Home

ALSO BY GIGI PRIEBE

The Adventures of Henry Whiskers

The Adventures of HENRY WHISKERS

By Gigi Priebe   Illustrated by Daniel Duncan

The Long Way Home

ALADDIN

New York   London   Toronto   Sydney   New Delhi

🪔 ALADDIN

An imprint of Simon & Schuster Children's Publishing Division
1230 Avenue of the Americas, New York, New York 10020
First Aladdin paperback edition August 2017
Text copyright © 2017 by Marjorie Priebe
Illustrations copyright © 2017 by Daniel Duncan
Also available in an Aladdin hardcover edition.
All rights reserved, including the right of reproduction in whole or in part
in any form.
ALADDIN and related logo are registered trademarks of Simon & Schuster, Inc.
For information about special discounts for bulk purchases, please contact Simon & Schuster Special Sales at 1-866-506-1949 or business@simonandschuster.com.
The Simon & Schuster Speakers Bureau can bring authors to your live event. For more information or to book an event contact the Simon & Schuster Speakers Bureau at 1-866-248-3049 or visit our website at www.simonspeakers.com.
Book designed by Laura Lyn DiSiena
The illustrations for this book were rendered digitally.
The text of this book was set in Vendome ICG.
Manufactured in the United States of America 0717 OFF
10 9 8 7 6 5 4 3 2 1
Library of Congress Control Number 2017945346
ISBN 978-1-4814-6578-6 (hc)
ISBN 978-1-4814-6577-9 (pbk)
ISBN 978-1-4814-6579-3 (eBook)

In memory of my parents,

Dolly & David Brush,

who modeled humility, community-mindedness,

respect for all, a sense of purpose,

and the spirit of adventure.

CONTENTS

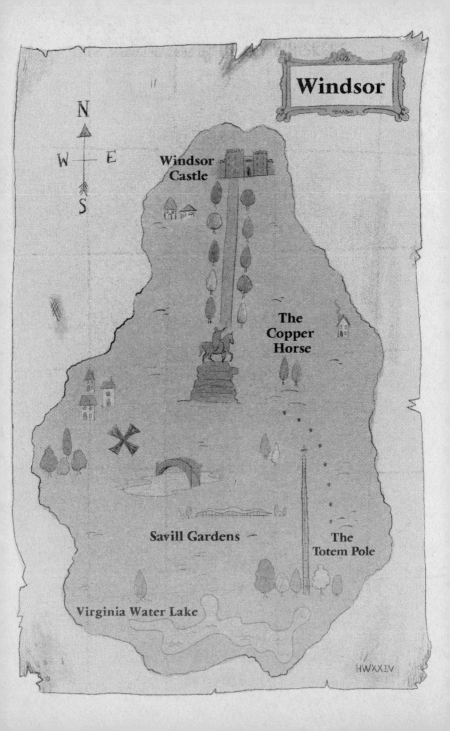

❖1❖
A MAP

HENRY WHISKERS SUCKED IN HIS BREATH and clamped a paw over his mouth. His rounded ears flicked back and forth, listening for any sign of trouble. Certain it was safe to continue, he raised the crumpled wad of paper to his nose and sniffed its musty nooks and crannies, then gently uncrinkled it and spread it out on the desk. His whiskers twitched with anticipation as he smoothed away its wrinkles. His heart ticked faster. This was *big*!

He could *feel* it! Right down to the tip of his tail.

A milky-white moon hung in the sky above Windsor Castle. Visitors and tour guides had long since gone home, including Warden, the tour guide in the exhibit room of the world's most famous dollhouse. Sitting on its base, raised to eye level for visitors to view, Queen Mary's Dollhouse glowed like a jewel in the middle of the dimly lit room. Standing five feet tall, eight feet long, and four feet wide, it made the perfect place for a family of mice to call home.

The night belonged to Henry! It was the *only* time Mother Mouse allowed him to roam the dollhouse and now he was convinced that he was onto *something*!

Only moments ago, he had been reading, sprawled across his favorite leather armchair in the library, when something had caught his eye. It was the shiny brass pulls on the desk drawers nearby. He had an idea. He lassoed the book with his tail, hopped out of the chair, and stuffed the book back into place on the bookshelf. On the desk there was a collection of fountain pens, leather-bound boxes, silver boxes, smoking pipes, and stationery. *Nothing can look out of place*, he reminded himself while his paws itched to touch each one of them.

Henry swung his tail out from under his charcoal-gray body and sat in the desk chair. He ran a forepaw across the smooth walnut-colored wood surface of the desk and noticed that the pens, letter openers, and a crystal bottle filled with blue ink were embossed with the queen's crown, just like the life-size versions that Her Royal Highness used. Photographs of people stood framed in sterling silver, smiling back at him. *It feels like they are watching me,* he thought as he clasped a shiny drawer pull and gave it a little tug. The drawer glided halfway out and got stuck. Upon inspection, Henry spied a piece of crumpled paper jammed in the back. Careful not to rip it, he eased it out. Flattened in front of him, he saw several scratchy paw-drawn images connected by lines and dots. Instantly he recognized the Copper Horse and the paved path leading up to it called the Long Walk. He'd seen them a hundred times from the castle's front windows. There were other things he didn't recognize, but they had words like *Totem Pole* and *Gardens* written next to them. To the left of all of the images, near the ragged edge, Henry noticed a large mysterious **X**.

Henry's heart thumped faster as he studied the map more closely. It nearly stopped when he spotted some small initials scratched on the lower right corner.

He slapped a paw over his mouth again. He could hardly contain himself. A flood of questions swirled through his mind. *How could he have . . . ? When did he . . . ? I wonder if . . . ? Does Mother . . . ?* Then it struck him. He had to show Jeremy. *Now!*

Henry swiftly rolled up the map and wound his tail around it. He slammed the desk drawer shut, leaped out of the chair, and shoved it back in its place. He gave the desk and the room one final inspection, then dashed off to find his best friend.

He's probably in the castle kitchens, Henry guessed, picturing Jeremy—who was also his distant cousin—nibbling away on crumbs from the queen's dinner much earlier that night. Henry hopped out of the dollhouse and onto the exhibit room floor. Navigating his way through the castle, he took all the shortcuts he knew, racing through the heating ducts until he reached Lantern Lobby just outside the biggest kitchen of them all. He poked his head out of a grate in the wall to check for Titus, the steely-eyed tabby cat who roamed around as if he owned the place. When Henry was certain that the coast was clear, he hopped out of the grate and darted across the floor toward the kitchen.

Twenty mouse lengths away from the kitchen door he planned to slip under, Henry heard a *clack-clack-clack*ing. It was the unmistakable sound of cat claws on the hard stone floor. Henry crouched, frozen to the spot, not daring to look or twitch a whisker. When he heard the clacking gather speed, he knew Titus had spotted him. Henry held his breath and made a run for it, slipping under the kitchen door just in time, leaving the nasty old fur ball hissing on the other side.

Henry sprang up onto all four paws as fast as he could and sprinted for cover under one of the massive, black iron ovens. He huffed and puffed until he caught his breath, then surveyed the enormous kitchen in search of Jeremy.

The floor was bathed in moonlight that poured

through the windows high above. Its gleam bounced off copper pots and kettles that lined the wall shelves and ringed the giant room. The very edges of the kitchen offered safe cover in the shadows cast by ovens, stoves, and worktables.

"Henry!" hollered Jeremy. "Over here!"

Henry turned toward the sound and eagerly waved the map for Jeremy to see, but Jeremy had turned away. Sitting in the middle of the open floor, spotlighted by moonglow, Jeremy looked like he didn't have a care in the world as he nibbled away on some whisker-wetting prize clutched in his oversized paws.

"Jeremy!" Henry yelled. "Look what I found!" He scampered out from cover and stopped to reconsider.

"Come on!" Jeremy was signaling for Henry to join him, but Henry shook his head. He was anxious to show Jeremy the map, but something told him to stay in the shadows.

Henry curled his tail around the map and made his way closer to Jeremy by hugging the wall under the ovens and stoves. When he was midway along, he cocked his ears and fixed his eyes on Jeremy. Something didn't feel right. "Jeremy," he shouted, but it was no use. Jeremy zigged and zagged back and forth across the floor following his nose in search of more crumbs. Henry shook his head, then all of a sudden, with no warning at all, the entire kitchen was flooded with bright fluorescent light.

Two cooks wearing white aprons, black-and-white checkered pants, and dark rubber-soled clogs marched in carrying cases that reminded Henry of suitcases from the dollhouse, just a whole lot bigger. Henry's heart leaped into his throat. He looked back and forth between the cooks and Jeremy, who had tucked himself into a tight ball below a table, just a few tail lengths away from one of the cook's feet. In the middle of the kitchen, there was nowhere to run without being seen. No wall to hug. No vent to hop into. No drain to duck down. No stove or refrigerator to hide under. Henry could hardly breathe. *Look at me, look at me,* he willed Jeremy, but at that very moment the black clog shifted and kicked Jeremy.

Jeremy shot out from under the table. The lady cook screeched and dropped her case, which crashed to the floor. An assortment of shiny, sharp kitchen knives—large and small—sprayed into the air and showered down all around Jeremy. He stopped still in his tracks.

Henry jumped out from under the stove. "Run, Jeremy. Run!"

Henry attempted to back up into the shadows again, but his legs felt heavy and wouldn't obey. The room began to swirl in front of his eyes as Jeremy stayed glued to the same spot, surrounded by knives.

Thwap! Whop! Whap! The familiar sound of a broom came close to Henry's head, blowing his whiskers back. Jeremy sprang in and out of Henry's view as he scampered, hopped, and skittered away from the attacking broom.

"Stop, you'll kill 'im," Henry heard the woman shriek.

"That's the idea, m'lady," the man shouted.

"Don't kill 'em, poor things. Let's trap 'em, and I'll trot 'em off tuh the park to set 'em free."

Henry's pulse pumped through his paws and pounded in his ears. Too stunned to move, he watched the lady cook lower a large metal mixing bowl over him. It all happened so fast, and yet it felt like slow motion. *CLANG!* The metal echoed as it hit the hard stone floor. Everything went dark except a thin ring of light that peeked under the rim.

✦2✦

FAR, FAR AWAY

SNAP OUT OF IT! HENRY ORDERED HIS body into action. He threw all his weight against the inside of the bowl, but it was no use. It wouldn't budge. He tried to hoist it up with his tail, but that didn't work either. He strained to hear what was happening around him.

It wasn't long before he heard the clink of metal on stone again. *Jeremy!* With the map still clasped in his paw, Henry was about to give the map a nervous nibble when he remembered its importance. He restrained himself and clutched it to his chest. His muscles thrummed in his legs, ready to run the first chance he got.

"Get me some cardboard," the lady's voice boomed above Henry.

The next thing Henry knew, the floor was moving—at least it seemed like it was. Something slid under the rim of the bowl and slipped from right to left, forcing him to hop onto it.

Swoop! Henry's stomach dipped as he felt himself lifted into the air. The bowl stayed firmly pressed down onto the cardboard he found himself standing on. Then suddenly, without warning, the bottom fell out.

Thud! Thankfully he landed on all four paws. The wind was knocked out of him and a hot flash of fear bolted through his body. In the glare of the bright light that hung overhead, he looked left and right to get his bearings. He was in a semi-transparent, milky-white container, so he could see shadowed figures moving beyond its four walls but nothing clearer than that.

With another thud, Jeremy landed next to him.

"Now what?" the male cook asked. "Why put them in there?"

"Because I have to drive them far away," said the lady cook. She spread something shiny that crinkled over the top of the container and molded it around the rim and outer walls, shading the interior.

"Drive them!" scoffed the other cook. "Since when do mice get driven?"

"Didn't you know that a mouse can find its way home from as far as a mile away?"

"You're pulling my leg," said the man doubtfully.

"It's true! So I'm going to take these two far, far

13

away and leave them somewhere nice so they can make a new life." The lady cook pricked lots of holes in the lid.

"I never knew that," he replied. "Now that you tell me, I bet I've been catching the same mouse over and over, but who knows." He chuckled. "All these rodents look the same to me."

Pressed against each other in a corner of the container, Henry could feel fear pulsing between them where his and Jeremy's hind haunches touched. And the look in Jeremy's eyes reflected the panic that Henry felt coiling deep in his stomach. He didn't like the sound of "very, very far away."

"That should do it!" The lady tapped the container gently. "I should be back in about twenty."

"Twenty what?"

"Twenty minutes."

"Blimey! Where are you taking them?

"Well . . ." The woman paused as if she was

still figuring that out. "If I'm going to make this much effort, I better drive them somewhere safe from people and cars. Maybe the park. How does Virginia Water Lake sound?"

"By golly!" said the man. "They're lucky you were the one to catch them. They'd be looking at the bottom of a garbage bin if it had been me."

Henry exchanged a wary look with Jeremy.

"Did you hear that guy?" Jeremy whispered. "He doesn't even know a mouse from a rodent!"

"We *are* rodents," murmured Henry. "All mice are."

"Oh," squeaked Jeremy.

Henry got the sinking feeling again when the lady lifted them up and carried them away. "See you soon," she hollered.

At least Jeremy's with me, thought Henry as they jiggled away.

A door banged shut and suddenly it was pitch black inside the container. Cold air poured through the air holes, sending shivers up Henry's spine. He tried to steady himself as the container rattled and the lady cook clomped along. After several minutes there was a creaky sound followed by a flash of light, another bang, total darkness, and a rumble that made everything shudder. With a sudden lurch, it felt like they were moving.

Things got really bumpy and swervy. Henry's and Jeremy's paws slipped out from under them as they slid from one side of the container to the other. There were more stops and starts than Henry could count, and then a violent jerk threw them in the air. Henry landed headfirst and Jeremy hurtled on top of him. All motion seemed to stop as they both rolled onto their backs.

"All right then, you two," said the lady. Something creaked again, the light came on, and Henry felt his stomach sink as they were lifted up. Something banged again and footsteps clomped on the ground for quite a ways. "This looks like a good spot," the lady said cheerfully after several minutes. She peeled back the crinkly lid and lowered her face so close that Henry could feel her warm breath when she spoke. "Oh, aren't you cute." She smiled, showing her large, crooked teeth.

Just then Henry noticed the pale rose color of sky above the woman's head and realized more time had passed than he'd imagined. Nighttime was giving way to dawn.

"Here you go," she said, bending over as she tipped the container upside down. Henry and Jeremy flopped out onto the cold, damp ground. "It's your lucky day," she said, turning to leave. "You can't possibly get into trouble now."

✦ 3 ✦
ONE TOO MANY

IN THE WOODEN BASE THAT QUEEN MARY'S Dollhouse rested on, and where the Whiskers family lived safely out of human sight, Mother Mouse glided across the kitchen floor. She counted the servings she had placed on the table. "Twelve, thirteen, fourteen..." Her shiny black paw stopped in midair. "Oh, crumpets!" she muttered to herself. She spun around to the counter behind her and scooped up one more helping of gooseberry seeds.

"Fifteen!" she said, piling them neatly at the end of the table and placing her paws on her slender hips.

Raising fifteen children by herself required the utmost organization. Raising them to be the next caretakers of the dollhouse and undetected by Warden and visitors of Windsor Castle required even more. Ever since her husband had died saving Mrs. Myrtle Mouse and her children from a fire, Mother Mouse depended heavily on her eldest children, Regina, Tudor, Thomas, James, Albert, Caroline, and Henry—maybe Henry the most. After all, he shared both his father's name and his sense of responsibility to Queen Mary's Dollhouse.

The dollhouse was never meant for dolls or even for children to play with. It works like a real home fit for a queen, complete with four floors, forty rooms, two working elevators, hot and cold running water, and electricity. Everything was made to be dollhouse-size, including a grand marble staircase, a kitchen with shiny copper pots, a garage filled with luxury cars, and toilets that really flush. Even crystal chandeliers that twinkle, a grandfather clock that chimes, and a library filled with leather-bound books were crafted like the life-size copies found in England's finest homes, so it's no wonder that nearly a million people come to see the dollhouse every year. But the one thing they've never seen are the mice that have nested among the empty cedar storage drawers built into the base. Twenty-four generations of Whiskers have nested there, tucked safely out of sight. Henry is the twenty-fifth in a long line of Henry Whiskers.

Mother Mouse liked to start her family's day with a healthy breakfast. After that, they were on their own to scour the kitchens, pantries, and banquet rooms of the queen's castle for their other meals, but not before completing their given chores. Chores were very important!

She clapped her paws and called everyone to the table. Isabel, the littlest and fastest, was first to skitter up and take her seat. Tudor, Thomas, James, Albert, Caroline, Mary, William, Victoria, Alexander, Charles, Beatrice, and Charlotte followed on her paws. Regina twirled in last while tying a pink satin ribbon around her neck.

One seat was empty. Had she miscounted? Mother Mouse looked at her children and noticed that Henry was missing. She shook her head and padded out of the kitchen, heading down the narrow hallway between each child's cedar drawer bedroom. She stopped at the entrance to Henry's room. "Henry?" she called softly, in case she was waking him. She poked her head inside. He wasn't there. *Humph,* she snuffed and padded back to the kitchen.

"Has anyone seen Henry this morning?" Mother Mouse asked. "Anyone?" she asked again when nobody answered.

"Not since last night," squeaked Albert, shoving some more gooseberry seeds in his mouth.

Heads nodded all around the table.

Mother went about her business, neatening up.

"He probably spent the night at Jeremy's," chirped Tudor.

"Or fell asleep you-know-where," Regina snickered, as if it would be typical of Henry to fall asleep in the library and risk being seen by Warden in the morning.

Mother Mouse waved off Regina's suggestion with her elegant paw while she picked up some stray crumbs and licked them from the other. "I don't think he's likely to do that again any time soon," replied Mother Mouse, recalling an earlier incident. *Henry's responsible,* she told herself. *He's not the one I need to worry about.*

When breakfast was over, Mother Mouse assigned chores for the day. "And when you are finished, would you run down to Aunt Begonia and Uncle Charlie's to see if Henry spent the night there with Jeremy?" She was looking at Regina when she asked the question.

"Ooh, you know I would, Mother, but I heard that the president of France and his wife are leaving today, and I had planned on nibbling a small swatch from one of her gowns before it gets packed." Regina batted her large brown eyes. "French fashions are the best, you know, so I would hate to miss the chance to get my paws on some."

"I wouldn't dream of such a thing," teased Mother Mouse, pretending to be shocked. "Be careful," she added in a more serious tone, then, turning to Tudor and Thomas, she asked "Would you two mind doing that for me? And if nobody's at home, drop by the King's Crumb. Henry could be there," she added as an afterthought. It wouldn't be surprising if Henry was helping Jeremy and

Uncle Charlie stock the shelves before the eatery opened up to the rest of the mouse community later that morning. "And no fooling around," she chided with her paws planted on her hips. "You two are still on probation!" Those were her final words of instruction before the kitchen emptied and she had the place to herself.

✦4✦
CLUELESS

SHAFTS OF BRILLIANT MORNING SUNLIGHT poked through fans of green ferns that swayed gently to and fro above Henry. *Am I dreaming?* he wondered. He shielded his eyes with a paw, accidentally knocking something next to him. Henry looked to his right to see what it was. "Jeremy!" Henry leaped up.

Jeremy sprang to his paws. His frightened eyes darted back and forth. "What happened?"

"We fell asleep! That's what!" Henry shook the fog from his head and rubbed his bleary eyes.

"Oy! I just remembered," Jeremy gasped. "What's this?" He dangled a crumpled piece of paper from one paw.

"The map!" Henry swiftly grabbed it from Jeremy. "This is what I wanted to show you when I came looking for you." He licked his dry lips. "I found it in the dollhouse library desk."

Jeremy eagerly snatched the map back. "Whoa!" His eyes widened as he examined the map, sniffing both sides and tracing the images with a paw. "Hey!" he squeaked. "What does that mean?"

"H-W-X-X-I-V." Henry read the letters out loud. "*H* is for Henry, *W* is for Whiskers, and the rest are Roman numerals for the number twenty-four."

"Wait," Jeremy began. "If you're the twenty-fifth Henry Whiskers, that means that this map—"

"Yep," Henry interrupted. "It belonged to my

26

father. But the thing is"—he scratched an ear—"I don't know when he could have made this."

"What do you mean?" asked Jeremy.

"I mean how could my father draw a map like this when he was a house mouse? He never lived out here." Henry looked at their strange surroundings and was reminded that they had no idea where they were. His stomach tightened as he glanced back over his shoulders in both directions.

"That's easy. He could see the Long Walk and the Copper Horse from the castle. He probably made up the rest," squeaked Jeremy, drawing Henry's attention back to the map.

Henry's paw skimmed over the images with words next to them. "I don't know. Why would he do that? And what's this big, fat ✖ for?"

"It's a mystery to me." Jeremy shrugged.

"That was kinda spooky," Henry squeaked.

"What are you talking about?"

"What you just said ... about a mystery." Henry paused, remembering. "My father used to tell me that the world is full of mysteries. I didn't really know what he meant, but I used to think it would be fun to find some."

"Well, I'd say this definitely counts as your first." Jeremy waved a paw through the air, drawing Henry's attention back to their unfamiliar surroundings.

"Where *are* we?" Henry gulped.

"Not a clue," squeaked Jeremy. "Except the cook said something about a park."

"Hmm."

Shaded woodland extended to either side of them and behind. Trees towered overhead. There was a paved path in front of them and people were strolling along. Beyond the path, some old stone ruins stood bathed in sunshine. Nearby Henry eyed some large clumps of tall reeds and grasses that bent in the breeze. Between the blowing blades of grass, something sparkled. He looked at Jeremy and tipped his head toward the spot. "Looks like a good place to hide, don't you think?"

Jeremy nodded. When all the people had passed, the two of them hightailed it into the open sunshine, across the paved path, and into the reeds. They paused to catch their breath.

Henry inched forward first, curious to see what was twinkling at him. Jeremy followed close on his paws. As the reeds thinned, Henry noticed a faint lapping sound that he didn't recognize. The light glared between the grasses, forcing Henry to shield his eyes and look down at the ground beneath his paws. All of a sudden the land dropped off steeply and he was falling—right into a huge lake!

✦ 5 ✦
DISTANT SHORE

THEY BOTH SHRIEKED JUST BEFORE THEY plunged into the cold water, tails first.

Splash! Splash!

Henry had the good sense to keep a tight grip on the map. When his hind paws touched bottom, he instinctively pushed off, thrusting himself back up. The second his snout rose to the surface he gulped for air.

At that very moment, a massive honey-colored

dog jumped into the lake—right near Henry and Jeremy! Waves washed over their heads, sweeping them further from the shore. Henry thrashed and kicked frantically, snatching small snouts full of air and looking for something to grab on to as he bobbed up and down. He saw Jeremy struggling to do the same.

"Mummy, look!" came a child's cry from the shore before another wave hit Henry in the face.

Henry pawed and paddled harder than ever until he found a rhythm: *Paddle, paddle, breathe. Paddle, paddle, breathe,* he commanded himself.

"Clover, come!" the mother called to the dog.

Paddle, paddle, breathe. He couldn't keep this up much longer.

The dog swam back to shore where Henry caught a glimpse of the small boy launching a bright red sailboat in their direction. It was their only chance.

31

"The boat," Henry sputtered. "Jeremy! Swim for the boat!"

Henry summoned all his strength and desperately pawed his way to the boat. When he was close enough, he cast his tail over its portside and held on tight while he extended a paw to Jeremy. "Grab hold. I'll pull you over."

It didn't take long to figure out that they couldn't both hang from the same side of the boat. Henry carefully clenched the soggy map in his teeth, then paw over paw he cautiously slid around to the opposite side from Jeremy so the boat would stay balanced. Over his shoulder, Henry saw the young boy jumping up and down, pumping the air with his fists, yelling, "Way 'ter go, mousies!"

Encouraged, Henry had an idea. "Jeremy," he called across the bow. "On the count of three, let's climb on board."

Jeremy managed a quick paws-up sign before clinging back to the boat.

"One . . . two . . . three!" Henry took a deep breath and hauled himself up and into the boat. He flopped onto his back, coughing and gasping for air. He heard a thump and knew that Jeremy was on board too.

For a long time the two of them lay there quietly, regaining their strength while the boat floated farther and farther away from shore. With his eyes closed, Henry felt the sun on his wet fur, warming his chilled body. It occurred to him that he might find this kind of fun if he weren't on a boat he couldn't sail, and completely lost! Just then he heard a spine-tingling screech above and his eyes popped open.

A large bird with thin brown stripes under its wings and across its chest was circling in the sky overhead. Henry's heart jumped into his throat as he watched the bird circle. "Do you think he eats mice?" Henry croaked.

"Do you think he sees us?" Jeremy whispered.

But before Henry had a chance to answer, the bird abruptly swooped down out of the sky. It swept low over the water and the boat, then soared up and away.

"That was too close," said Jeremy. "Did you see the beak on that guy?"

Henry's heart was thumping. "I think it's a sparrow hawk. I've seen pictures in a book." He hesitated, then suddenly remembered: "They *do* eat mice!" A horrible image flashed through Henry's head, but just as he was picturing being eaten by the bird, the hint of an idea popped into his head. He sat bolt upright, as if he might catch it before it disappeared. The boat tipped violently.

"What are you doing?" hollered Jeremy.

Henry grabbed hold of the mainsail and sat very still until the rocking stopped.

"Did you hear me?" asked Jeremy.

"No."

"Why not?"

"I was working on an idea," said Henry.

"About what?"

"About how to find our way home."

Now Jeremy sat up. "I'm all ears. What are you thinking?"

"I'm not sure. That's as far as I got." But Henry felt like a glimmer of a plan might still be brewing in the back of his mind. He squeezed his eyes shut and concentrated.

"Let's look at the map!" Henry opened his eyes and smoothed out the soggy map, being careful not to tear it.

"We don't even know if we are anywhere *on* this map," scoffed Jeremy.

"True." Henry's whiskers drooped. "But it's all we've got." He looked at Jeremy.

Jeremy shrugged.

"I know!" Henry perked up. "We'll do what Mother Mouse always says. We'll go as far as we can see and when we get there, we will be able to see farther."

Jeremy looked doubtful, but Henry directed his attention to the mainsail. "All right then. That's the spirit!" Henry stood up very slowly and held on to the mainsail to keep his balance. Jeremy did the same. With the two of them standing on either side, they scanned the horizon. Where it didn't sparkle with the sun's reflection, the lake looked dark and deep…like it wanted to swallow them up. It was so long that they couldn't see either end of it. They were floating in the middle. Thick woods lined the shore behind them while large patches of red, white, and pink flowering bushes painted the gently sloping hills on the shore in front. In the hollows of the hills, pools of yellow daffodils floated on blankets of new spring-green grass. To the far right of the hills, leafy trees and tall pines spread as far as Henry and Jeremy could see.

"Hold the mast and keep the boat steady while I climb up there and take a look." He pointed at the map. "And keep a paw on that so it doesn't blow overboard."

Jeremy clamped a hind paw down on the map and clasped the mast firmly between his front paws. "Aye, aye, Captain!" Jeremy grinned at Henry, spreading his hind legs for balance and leaning against the mast while Henry shinnied up it.

When Henry reached the top, he sniffed in every direction. He could practically taste the sweet smells that wafted through the air. "The wind's at our backs," he hollered down to Jeremy, "and pushing us straight for those hills. With a little luck, I think we'll make the far shore by midday."

Just as he was about to slide down to the main deck, something caught Henry's eye. He blocked the glare of the sun with his paw and scanned the horizon. Peeking out just above the pines he noticed something odd. The longer he looked the more familiar it became.

Suddenly he knew why.

✦ 6 ✦
EYE SPY

HENRY SCRAMBLED DOWN THE MAINSAIL
to the deck below.

"Whoa! What's the hurry?" hollered Jeremy, trying to steady the rocking boat.

"Climb up there and tell me what you see!"
Henry panted. "Over in that direction," he added,
pointing impatiently toward the distant trees.

Jeremy clung to the mainsail and shook his

head. "Don't like all this rocking. Not a good idea! Let's just keep our paws put!"

"I think I saw something that's on the map!" Henry waved off Jeremy's paw to inspect the map. His whiskers twitched as he held the map flat. Parts of it were blurry, where the water made the ink run. Henry's gaze hovered briefly over the mysterious ✖ before he spotted what he was looking for.

"That's it!" Henry pointed at an image with the words below that said *Totem Pole*.

Jeremy's eyes bulged.

"You know what that means, right?" Henry asked, clapping his paws. He didn't wait for Jeremy's answer. "If I'm right, that means that this is a map of Windsor Great Park!" Henry shook his head in disbelief.

"Why does it mean that? We could be in any park." Jeremy scratched his ear, confused.

"Because," said Henry, sticking up one paw, "we can see the Copper Horse statue from the castle, which we know is in Windsor Great Park. And two"—he stuck up his other paw—"if it's on the map and the totem pole is on the same map, this has to be a map of the same park." Henry crossed his forelegs. "That's the park the lady cook meant."

Neither spoke as they tried to make sense of it all.

"Maybe we're not as far from home as we thought," said Jeremy, sounding like he only half believed it.

"Well . . ." Henry drew a long breath and began. "'The Long Walk leads into five thousand acres of land that was once hunted on by kings of England hundreds of years ago.'" Henry recited the words as well as any one of the Windsor Castle tour guides, which he had heard countless times. But he had no idea how far and wide five thousand acres spread.

"Maybe we'll see home if we climb to the top of the totem pole?" Henry wondered out loud, feeling hopeful.

Just then a strong breeze whipped across the lake and nearly capsized the boat. If he hadn't been holding on to the mainsail Jeremy would have been thrown overboard. The water rippled and the boat tossed back and forth.

"Quick! Over here!" Henry hollered, waving Jeremy over to his side of the boat. But before Jeremy could make a move, another gust of wind blew from behind and sent the boat rocketing across the wavy water. Henry grabbed the map and clutched it tightly with his tail.

"Judging by the wind in my whiskers and the speed of the boat," Jeremy shouted, " I think we're going to hit land hard."

"Hold tight!" yelled Henry. "Rough landing ahead!"

Henry hastily rolled the map and clenched it in his teeth before he and Jeremy braced themselves as best as they could by wrapping their tails around the mainsail and clutching the sides of the boat with their paws. Where the water ran shallow, the boat scraped over jagged rocks. The decking beneath their paws ripped open and Henry fell through. He was waist-high in cold water but still holding on with one paw. The boat dragged him along until the bow crashed into the bank of the lake with a violent jerk and crumpled.

"We're taking on water!" yelled Jeremy.

"Hurry, or she'll take us down with her," Henry hollered back.

The two of them pawed their way out of the sinking boat as fast as they could. They crawled up the dirt bank and collapsed on soft blades of grass at the top.

Drenched to the bone, Henry spit out the

map, rolled onto his back and flung all four paws out. Breathing hard he stared up at the sun high in the sky. "Whew! What a ride!" He began to chuckle with relief when he had an eerie flash-back of the hawk swooping down toward them. He shook it off.

Jeremy coughed up some water and joined in, laughing so hard that he could barely get the words out: "No ... body"—cough—"is ..."—cough—"going to believe this."

"We've got to find that totem pole before it gets too late," Henry chirped, hoisting himself up onto all four paws. He shook water from his coat and smoothed his tangled whiskers. Careful not to rip the map, he refolded it and tucked it in his paw.

"We better go," Jeremy squeaked.

Henry followed his instincts. Jeremy followed Henry. "If we stick to the paved people path, it might lead us to the pole," said Henry, sounding more confident than he felt.

The sweet-scented flowering bushes and daffodils in the open meadows were well behind them. Here in the woods, tall trees towered high overhead, shading the cool ground beneath their paws. The smell of damp soil, pine needles, and last year's leaves filled their nostrils.

The longer they trudged along, the more Henry thought about home. He missed the sugary smells from Mother Mouse's kitchen and the sounds of his sisters and brothers chasing after one another throughout the dollhouse. He even missed the castle cat! Henry laughed.

"What's so funny?" grumbled Jeremy.

"I was just thinking of all the things I miss about home."

"What's funny about that?"

"Titus!" snickered Henry. "I never thought I'd miss *him*!"

"At least with Titus we know what we're up against," Jeremy muttered.

Henry felt a prickle at the back of his neck. He smiled warily back at Jeremy as he recalled the near-death encounter they once had with Titus.

He knew what Jeremy meant. They didn't know what to expect in the wilds ... who to trust or how to find their way in this new world.

As they scampered along, Henry heard an unfamiliar buzzing sound. It came and went as if carried by the breeze.

"Did you hear that too?" asked Jeremy, who must have noticed Henry looking around.

"Where's it coming from?"

They both stopped when the sound returned. Suddenly, before they knew what was happening, they were dive-bombed by several fuzzy, yellow-and-black–banded bugs with long, pointy stingers. *Bzzzzzzzzz!*

"Yow! Let's get out of here," hollered Henry, gripping the map and darting away. He ran toward higher ground, where there was a clear path to the giant pole that now loomed black against the dusky sky.

"What are you thinking?" panted Jeremy by his side.

"We're losing the sun," Henry groaned. "We're going to be too late to see anything from the top." A wave of panic rose in the pit of Henry's stomach.

"You were right," said Jeremy when they finally reached the totem pole.

The two of them tilted their heads up to the sky where orange-gray clouds swept past the top of the totem pole. On the ground, the woods had turned black and unfamiliar sounds rang out all around them.

"You know what this means, don't you?" Henry worried, kicking the dirt beneath his paws.

Jeremy nodded, looking as frightened as Henry felt.

"We better look for somewhere safe to sleep," Henry whispered.

WHAT TO BELIEVE

IT WASN'T UNUSUAL FOR HENRY TO SLEEP over at Jeremy's without telling Mother Mouse, but when Tudor and Thomas reported that neither their brother nor Jeremy had spent the night there, she got a pit in her stomach.

That was several hours ago, she realized as the day wound down and there was still no sign of Henry. She nervously tapped her tail on the floor. "That's it! I can't wait any longer," she muttered. She stroked the sore tip of her silky tail with a paw, then sprinted up a well-worn path from the cedar storage drawers into the dollhouse. She ducked inside the chimney and scaled up to the library. She didn't dare hop out onto the exposed floor until she checked to be sure the coast was clear. On rare occasions the castle stayed open late for special groups of visitors, so tour guides such as Warden and visitors alike could still be walking about the exhibit room. A mouse in the house would most certainly catch their attention.

Mother Mouse held her breath and cocked her ears from inside the chimney. Sure enough, she heard familiar footsteps as they slowly circled around the house, then faded away toward the entrance to the room. That was Warden's routine. Mother Mouse knew it well. He would greet visitors at the doorway to the exhibit room, and if the lines of visitor trickled down to a slow stream, he would pace around the house. On evenings when they stayed open late he would adjust the lighting in the exhibit hall to make sure the dollhouse sparkled like a jewel in the center of the room.

As the sound of Warden's footsteps faded into the distance, Mother Mouse was certain that Henry wasn't there—at least not in sight—but she couldn't think of anything better to do, so she told herself *I should double-check, just in case.* She poked her head out from the chimney. She scampered onto the library rug and stood on her hind legs to get a better view of the surrounding room. Her whiskers twitched nervously as she eyed the bookshelves. *Good!* She sighed. *Everything looks in place.*

She was just about to hop back into the chimney when she happened to glance over at the desk. Instantly her pulse quickened and she caught her breath. She didn't know why, exactly, but she was overcome by a sudden feeling of dread.

"Good evening, ladies and gentlemen," Warden said, startling Mother Mouse.

She cast a glimpse back over her shoulder and saw him welcoming a cluster of tourists.

"For the safety of the exhibit," Warden continued, "would you please park your umbrellas in the bins?"

It's now or never, Mother Mouse thought. Moving swiftly, she scanned the desk for anything that might be out of place. *Frames, pens, ink, blotter, books, boxes. . . .* She eyed each one, making sure that none was crooked or out of position. Satisfied, she quickly checked the drawer. It was open just a crack.

"That's it, then. Thank you all for your cooperation," she heard Warden saying to the visitors as they walked into the room.

She had to act fast. Mother Mouse pulled the chair away from the desk and gently slid the desk drawer open. She tilted her head to peek inside. *Envelopes, notepaper, and . . .* her heart skipped a beat. She stood up and pulled the drawer all the way open. She had to be sure. *No map!*

"Please don't touch," Warden said to the little group as they approached the dollhouse.

Mother Mouse promptly shut the drawer, ducked under the desk, pulled the chair back in, and disappeared into the darkened chimney. She was certain nobody saw her, but nevertheless, she felt a prickle at the back of her neck the whole way home. She kept telling herself, *Henry wouldn't go without telling me first. He just wouldn't.*

If only she could convince herself that it were true.

◆8◆
THE TOTEM POLE

AS HARD AS HE TRIED, HENRY COULD NOT sleep. Terrifying night sounds sharpened his senses and echoed within the hollow tree trunk where he and Jeremy had taken shelter. He'd force his eyelids shut, but they'd snap back open with every hoot or holler that haunted the night. He tossed and turned on a bed of brittle leaves, wishing daylight would come faster. He longed for his soft, warm bed of cotton balls and cattail fluff, which only made the ground beneath him feel that much harder.

Without warning the wind picked up and it began to rain. Jeremy rustled nearby.

"Are you awake?" Henry whispered, but his words were swallowed by the rising storm. He asked again, louder this time.

"Who can sleep?" Jeremy practically shouted as wind-whipped rain pelted the ground and rattled tree branches outside the hollow.

The two of them burrowed deeper into the tree trunk's crannies and stayed like that—tails tucked tightly under them through most of the night. Sometime near dawn the wind stopped howling, the branches stopped clattering, and the rain stopped splattering.

Just when the world outside the hollow had finally begun to lighten, Henry could hardly keep his eyes open and he slipped off into a fitful sleep filled with frightening images of unknown crea-tures. He dreamed he was back in the lake, struggling against a powerful current, when all of a sudden he felt an icy-cold shock ripple through his paws and he woke with a jolt.

A stream of frigid rainwater had trickled into the hollow and was pooling around the two of them. Henry sprang into the air. Jeremy did the same, with hardly a second between sleep and alert wakefulness.

"Let's get out of here!" said Henry, holding the map high in the air and cocking his head toward the opening.

"I'm right behind you," squeaked Jeremy as he followed Henry out into the soggy world beyond.

Henry ran straight back to the totem pole. He looked up to the sky, sniffed the air, and said, "Race you to the top."

"Wait!" said Jeremy, holding Henry back. "Tell

me what that says." He pointed at a large sign planted in front of the totem pole.

Henry cast a cautious eye out to check for humans or other unwanted visitors before he turned and focused on the giant words in front of them. With no one in sight, he skittered closer to the sign and sounded out the unfamiliar words.

"This totem pole was a gift to Her Majesty the Queen from the people of Canada."

"Where's that?" asked Jeremy.

Henry stroked his whiskers, wondering the same thing. Suddenly a memory flashed in his mind. "You know that spinning ball in the library . . . the one with a map of the world on it?" Henry didn't wait for an answer. "Canada is near the top . . . like right above America." Henry paused, remembering when Father Mouse had once explained the curious map and places on it. *How did he know so much?* Henry was wondering when Jeremy nudged him to keep reading.

"The pole is one hundred feet tall and weighs…" His words trailed off. Henry had never seen a number with so many zeros. He pointed a paw at it and looked to Jeremy for help.

"Whoa!" gasped Jeremy. "Twenty-seven thousand pounds. That's *humungous*!"

Henry peered up at the giant pole before he read a little more. "So it says that this tree was six hundred years old when it was cut down and the carvings are in the style of the Pacific Coast tribes. There's a carving of a man with a hat on his head at the very top, a beaver, a whale, a …" But before Henry could finish, Jeremy tore off to get a head start. "Bet I'll beat you to the top," Jeremy hollered over his shoulder.

"Not if I beat you first." Henry lassoed the map in his tail and raced after Jeremy.

They both shinnied up the pole as fast as they could. The climb was straight and steep, and after several minutes Henry noticed that they had both slowed down. Every time he peered up at the top, it seemed no closer, so he decided to play a game with himself. He hummed a little tune to the rhythm of his paws. *Right paw, left paw, huff and puff. Right paw, left paw, rough and tough.* He tried to change the words that rhymed with huff and puff, but he ran out after *had enough*, which seemed like a good place to stop anyway.

Henry was rather enjoying himself when Jeremy yelled from the other side.

"Don't look down."

That just made Henry want to look. *Ugh!* That was a mistake. Instantly he felt woozy. When he checked the distance to the top again, he realized that they were more than halfway up.

"Hey, since you're so good with numbers," he

shouted back to Jeremy, "how far up do you think we are?"

"Well," Jeremy huffed, climbing paw over paw, "if we are three quarters of the way, and three quarters of one hundred is seventy-five, we must be seventy-five feet high and have twenty-five feet left to go." He paused. "By my calculations, that means we have another two hundred tail lengths left."

"Sorry I asked," puffed Henry.

Just then a gust of wind forced Henry and Jeremy to stop and cling tight. Henry scrunched his eyes closed and counted. He counted as high as he could, to one hundred, three times over before the wind died down. When he opened his eyes again, the top of the pole was wrapped in a golden glow from the sun.

"That was a whisker-whipper," cried Jeremy.

"We're almost there," Henry yelled back before

shinnying the last several mouse lengths up and onto to the top.

They didn't dare stand on their hind legs in case of another gust, but they didn't need to.

"No wonder they call it Great Park," Jeremy squeaked in awe.

From the top of the pole they looked out onto a sea of trees. Young spring leaves seemed to wave at them in the breeze. Carefully Henry and Jeremy circled the top of the pole, searching the horizon.

"This is no better than being down on the ground," muttered Henry, slumping his shoulders. He unfolded the map and held it tight so it wouldn't blow away. "I still can't see anything that might lead us closer to home."

"What are we looking for?"

"I don't know." Henry tapped his tail nervously. "I was hoping we'd see the Copper Horse from here."

"There's the lake," Jeremy pointed behind them.

"It's on the map," said Henry, "but I can't tell which direction we're looking. Wait! I know." Henry's heart skipped. He realized how to tell which way they were facing as he held the map in front of them. "Look," he said, pointing to the sky. "The sun rose over there this morning and it's moving across the sky from right to left. That means east is to our right and west is to our left." He waved his paw like a wand through the air.

"And that means north is that way"—Henry pointed away from the lake—"and south is over there."

"So what," said Jeremy. "How does that help?"

Henry held out the map. "If the Long Walk and the Copper Horse are south of the castle, and the totem pole is even further south, then home must be that way," explained Henry, pointing in the air again. "We just have to keep going away from the lake and up that hill over there." Henry checked the map again. "Father Mouse made dots from the totem pole that lead that way too." A wave of relief washed over Henry.

Jeremy smiled. "Makes sense to me. Just hope we get to sleep in our own beds tonight."

The idea of another night in the wilderness was more than Henry could think about. A shiver crept up his spine, and he tried to push the thought from his mind.

As the two of them gazed out on the park from the top of the totem pole, a red balloon caught Henry's eye. It broke away from a young child and was being carried by the breeze—low to the ground at first, then up and up. As Henry tracked its course, it passed over a dirt path that led up a hill and disappeared into the trees. "Look!" he nudged Jeremy. "That's where we want to aim for."

Jeremy high-pawed Henry. "Let's go!"

⇥ 9 ⇤

DIVIDE AND CONQUER

BY THE TIME THEIR PAWS HIT THE GROUND, Henry was determined to get home before dark. "We've got to keep moving," he said, not wasting a second before dashing off toward the red balloon that he saw stuck in a tree. Jeremy followed close behind. When they reached the tree with the balloon at the top of a hill, the path they were on forked off in two different directions. They stopped to catch their breath and get a lay of the land.

"Which way?" chirped Jeremy.

Henry glanced at the map. "I can't tell if these dots follow the paths, or if they are a trail that Father Mouse blazed by himself."

"We could split up and scout in different directions," Jeremy suggested. "Then we'd cover twice as much ground in the same amount of time and double our chances of finding the right path home."

"I like the way you think," said Henry, smacking his tail on Jeremy's back. "Okay, you go that way"—he pointed west toward a large hedge—"and I'll go north through those trees. We'll meet back here under the hedge before the sun's slanty in the sky. That should give us enough time, don't you think?" Henry twirled a few whiskers as he pondered. "But what if we get lost and can't find our way back?"

"Good point," said Jeremy. "We could leave a

trail." He clapped his paws. "How about some of these?" He picked up an acorn and held it up.

When they couldn't hold any more acorns, they reviewed the plan and set off in different directions. At first Henry was excited, but the longer he was by himself—alone—the more anxious he got. He reminded himself to toss an acorn now and then and look back at the way he'd come so he could remember it later, he hoped.

Henry reached a clearing where the trees gave way to sweeping open spaces that were carpeted in green and blanketed by sun. His nose alerted him to the gardens beyond before his eyes spotted them. Buds were bursting and blossoming every-where he looked. The smells of cherry blossom, tulips, dogwood, and magnolia mixed in the air and tickled his nose. Henry closed his eyes and took a long, deep breath. For a brief moment he almost forgot about his worries while he soaked in the sun and sweet smells surrounding him.

When it seemed safe, Henry ventured across the open lawn and hopped into a large bed of daffodils. He tucked himself deep into the center of the flowerbed. *Keep going,* he told himself. He worked his way through the daffodils and poked his head out when he reached more lush green lawn on the far side. It wound its way between swirling, curving beds of multicolored flowers. Along one side of the giant garden was a silver-gray building with a wavy-shaped roof, glass walls, and a long deck that overlooked the gardens. A sign next to it read SAVILL GARDENS. *Not on the map!* He double-checked. *But wait! The map did say "gardens." Maybe this was the same spot after all.* Henry scratched behind an ear and let the thought roll around in his mind for a moment.

The familiar smell of scones and clotted cream caught his attention. His stomach rumbled and grumbled. Temptation tickled his whiskers, but looking at the sun Henry knew time was running out, and he decided to get back to Jeremy.

Just as Henry turned to meet back up with Jeremy, he caught sight of a sandy-brown field mouse perched on a toadstool not far from the gray building in Savill Garden. It looked like he was teaching a class to a dozen younger looking mice clustered in front of him. They sat wide-eyed, listening obediently. Henry cocked an ear toward them and strained to listen.

"First thing in the morning is no good," the bigger mouse told them. "The decks get swept clean, so it's not worth the effort. Your best bet is to wait until after those folks munch on lunch and take afternoon tea. That's when you'll get the most crumbs for your caper." He pointed a paw back over his shoulder for everyone to notice the swarm of people having their tea at picnic tables on the deck.

"Where do they take it?" squeaked one of them. Her petite paws and pink ears briefly reminded Henry of his littlest sister, Isabel.

"To the Queen of England," squeaked another, rolling his eyes in the back row.

They all began to giggle and elbow one another. The older-looking mouse smiled patiently and waited until they were quiet again.

"Perfectly good question, Lily," he said. "But they don't take their tea anywhere. It's what humans say when they mean that they are going to drink tea and eat a snack."

"I like snacks," bellowed one of the mice.

"We all like snacks, Dimwood," said the sandy-brown mouse. "That's why we're here." He turned and pointed at the flowerbeds right in front of the deck. "It's usually best to approach from over there," he continued, pointing to the far end of the deck. "That way we can work from one end to the other in a straight line and you won't miss anything. But if you ever have to make a fast escape, you can jump into those flowers where you won't be seen. From there you can wait it out or slip under the deck. No one will chase you there."

By the time he'd answered everyone's questions and they had reviewed their strategy, the tea-takers were beginning to leave. The bigger mouse clapped his paws together and said, "Right-o! Are you ready?"

Henry would have stayed to ask the mice for help, but he didn't dare risk further delay. He had to get back to Jeremy, but as he turned to go, he hoped that help would wait for them.

✦ 10 ✦
THINGS ARE LOOKING UP

JEREMY WAS ALREADY WAITING IN THE hedge when Henry ran up to him.

"What did you find?" panted Henry.

"Just a lot more trees." Jeremy sounded discouraged.

"Well, it's not on the map," Henry said with a smile, "but I found something that will make you happy. Can you guess?"

"Mum's blueberry crumb cakes," Jeremy said sarcastically. "I'm starved!"

"Close. Follow me." And with that Henry led Jeremy back to Savill Garden, where the air smelled sweet and a banquet of tasty tidbits awaited them.

Henry pointed out the building where the last people to go disappeared through a doorway, leaving the deck and all its fresh morsels ready to sample. There was no sign of the other mice.

"Things are looking up." Jeremy beamed at Henry, sounding like his happy old self again. He was about to dash to the deck when Henry held him back.

"Wait!" Henry warned. "Keep an eye out for that hawk we saw earlier. Let's stay close to cover." Then Henry thought about what he'd overheard the field mouse say. "We'll work our way down the deck. At the first sign of trouble, jump into that flowerbed next to it."

Jeremy nodded with a mischievous gleam in his eye. "Okay." He took half a hop out of the flowerbed into the clearing, cast a quick eye at the sky, then shot out into the open, covering the distance between the daffodils and the deck in no time flat. Henry shook his head and raced after Jeremy, just as eager to put his paws on some moist munchies and fill his empty stomach.

✦ 11 ✦
SEARCH PARTIES

MOTHER MOUSE GATHERED EVERYONE IN the kitchen and told them the plan. She had hardly slept the night before, but forced herself to sound upbeat and matter-of-fact. *No time for tears,* she told herself.

"I don't want to scare you," she started. "I'm sure Henry and Jeremy are fine, but I would feel better if I knew where they are, so I would like you all to help."

"Tudor," she said with her no-messing-around voice. "You and Thomas go check for Henry and Jeremy at the Neighborhood Nibble. Even if they aren't there, be sure to ask if anyone has seen them."

"Regina, I want you and Caroline to swing by the King's Crumb and ask Uncle Charlie if Jeremy returned since we last checked."

"What about my French fabric?" Regina squeaked desperately.

Mother Mouse stiffened. Impatience flashed in her eyes and her whiskers bristled.

"All right! All right!" Regina surrendered.

Mother Mouse wrung her paws before she handed out her next assignment. "Isabel, can you remember how to find Rat Alley?"

"I think so."

Mother Mouse smiled to herself. "You're getting so big," she said, padding over to her youngest. She stroked the back of Isabel's silky, soft head.

"Can you show James and Albert the way?"

James and Albert flashed a worried look at each other as Mother Mouse faced them. "The Lower Ward in the underground tunnels?" James croaked.

Albert chimed in. "You mean that stinky place where you forbid us to go and mice are mouse munch if they're caught?"

Mother Mouse clasped her paws and took a slow, deep breath. "Sometimes we have to bend the rules. Just stay away from Snag and that rat pack of his." Mother Mouse tried to sound reassuring. "Henry and Jeremy might have gone to visit Silver Snout." She was talking about the wise elder rat that Henry and Isabel befriended once when they got lost in Rat Alley. She prayed that this was where they had gone. "Be careful," she warned. "Isabel can guide you."

"Yeah! Just follow me." Isabel beamed proudly.

"You're a brave girl." Mother Mouse leaned over

and gave her a nuzzle. "And sneaky, too," she added. "I know you'll be careful. And I know that your brothers will keep an eye out for trouble. You won't be alone."

James and Albert exchanged another anxious look, then puffed out their chests and waved their paws in the air. "Lead the way," squeaked Albert as he and James fell in line behind Isabel.

"Wait!" Mother Mouse held up a paw. "I want you all to come straight back here as fast as you can. No lingering or stopping to see friends. There's plenty of time for that later." She crossed her forepaws and looked straight at Tudor and Thomas.

"We will," they all promised before bounding out of the kitchen.

Mother Mouse waved them good-bye and collapsed on a stool when they were out of sight.

"What about us?" squeaked Charlotte, standing with her younger littermates.

Mother Mouse turned to her youngest children. Worry weighed on their whiskers as they stared wide-eyed back at her. "You're not old enough," she said faintly at the very moment she realized that she'd just sent Isabel, the youngest of them all. She hoped she hadn't just made a terrible mistake.

☙ 12 ☙
TEA TIME

WHILE HENRY AND JEREMY SNIFFED OUT savory crumbs beneath the picnic tables, Henry spied the group of field mice he had seen earlier. They were working their way closer from the opposite end of the deck. He hadn't noticed the others in their midst until a fleeting shadow caught his attention and he looked up. He stopped nibbling midchew and sat up on his hind legs. His heart skipped a beat. "Psst," he whispered, hoping only Jeremy could hear him.

Jeremy stopped and looked at Henry. He followed Henry's gaze toward the other mice. "Field mice?" Jeremy wondered out loud. "Where did they come from?" He cocked his ears and sat high on his haunches, watching cautiously.

"Saw them earlier," whispered Henry. "Don't know if this is their turf," he added.

The two of them sat at attention, waiting to be noticed and ready to run if they had to. Even the younger looking field mice were bigger than Henry and Jeremy, with sandy-brown fur, light gray underbellies, and slightly larger ears. It didn't take long to be noticed.

It was the leader of the group that saw them first. He popped up on hind paws and watched Jeremy and Henry intently through large, protruding eyes. He couldn't have been more than a hundred paw prints away, which was nothing given the speed of a mouse. Stiff whiskered and poised to run, Henry studied him closely, looking for a sign, anything that would tell him if the other mouse was friend or foe. He didn't dare blink.

One by one, the younger field mice stopped in their tracks to stare. Henry could practically feel all twenty-six curious eyes on him. Nobody twitched. As far as Henry could tell, the other mice seemed just as surprised and were probably equally harmless. He took a chance. Cupping his paws around his mouth, he hollered, "Looks like plenty for everyone." Henry noticed the whiskers on the bigger mouse relax and a faint smile curl his lips. With a wave of his paw, the younger ones returned to their scavenging and the bigger one did too.

Henry nudged Jeremy with an elbow and they set back to sniffing and snuffling. As they followed the trail of crumbs, they found themselves mingling among the others. It happened quietly ... without any fanfare, hellos, or how-do-you-dos, but now and then they would catch one another's eye and exchange timid smiles.

Just when Henry was thinking that the mice reminded him of his own sisters and brothers, he got the feeling he was being watched.

♦ 13 ♦
A BIRD'S-EYE VIEW

HENRY SPUN AROUND AND SPOTTED THE
sparrow hawk just before it slipped from sight
between the branches of a nearby tree. He sat
alert and upright while all the other mice kept
their noses to the ground, unaware of the danger
that lurked close by. When several minutes passed
without any sign of the bird, Henry thought he'd
sneak a few more crumbs before calling it quits.

The second he felt a sudden burst of wind

behind him, Henry realized his mistake. He turned just in time to see two curved claws aiming straight for them.

Without even thinking, Henry threw himself on top of the closest mouse in order to protect him. The next thing he knew, his chest felt as if it might collapse and air was being squeezed out of him. With a vicious yank he was swept into the sky at stomach-churning speed.

Helpless, Henry gasped for air. Each tiny breath triggered a sharp pain that ran from his chest to the very end of his long, limp tail. The hawk sliced through the air at tremendous speed, while Henry's whiskers whipped against his cheeks and his eyes watered.

You're alive, Henry told himself. *Keep breathing.... Ouch ... Don't try to wriggle.... That hurts.... Open your eyes.... Watch where you're going.*

When it felt as if they were gliding through the

air, Henry forced himself to open his eyes. The world was far, far below, and it seemed like they were flying in large circles, as if the bird didn't know where it wanted to go with its newfound prize.

Everything looked so small from up so high. Even the statue of the Copper Horse looked miniature.

Wait a minute! Henry craned his neck, squinting intently as they flew by. *It IS the Copper Horse. . . .* His heart pounded against his aching ribs. *And if that's the Copper Horse, then . . .* Just then the bird banked hard to the left and Henry lost sight of the one thing familiar to him. *Please . . . please . . . ,* he begged, hoping the bird would fly over the spot again.

Swoop . . . swirl . . . *flap, flap,* glide . . . *whoosh.*

It took every ounce of Henry's strength to concentrate. He tried his hardest to study the landscape below, and as he did, it became clearer somehow, all spread out *like the map!* He suddenly saw how everything connected: the giant lake, gardens, the forest, the totem pole, and . . .

Flap, flap, glide . . . *flap, flap,* glide. The bird banked back the other way.

There it is again . . . the greenish-black statue of a horse with a rider on top. Through tear-filled eyes he spied what he was searching for. *I see it!* he thought. *The long walk . . . rows of trees to either side . . . and . . .* his eyes traced the long walk to its distant end and there was . . . *HOME!* Windsor Castle, plain as day— enormous compared to everything next to it.

Henry's stomach suddenly lurched as the bird plummeted downward. *He's going to pick me apart or swallow me whole for supper,* thought Henry. His mind raced as they swept over treetops, back the way they'd come.

Henry spied the gardens and the wavy-shaped roof growing larger as they neared. Beyond the gardens he caught sight of mice. They looked too small for Henry to tell if Jeremy was with them ... more like a string of dark dots snaking across a green open space heading toward a stream with a bridge across it. That's all he saw before the hawk pumped its wings, *one, two, three* times, then swiftly glided through the trees. Henry felt dizzy. He closed his eyes tight and held his breath.

All he could do was hope.

⇥ 14 ⇤
ESCAPE

THE BIRD FLEW THROUGH THE TREES AT such speed it made Henry feel sick. He couldn't watch any more for fear that he would be struck by a branch and ripped from the bird's sharp talons. Instead, and without any warning, Henry felt himself falling, free from the claws and their viselike grip. He landed on his back with a *thwunk*. A shot of pain seared through his body.

Henry's eyes popped open. *Where's the bird?*

He searched the tangle of tree limbs above him. *Where is he? Probably waiting . . . going to pounce and eat me alive!* He blinked. *Nowhere!*

Henry slowly turned his head from side to side. As he reached a paw out to inspect the twigs woven in front of him, he saw the map still clenched in it.

Careful. Don't snag it. He forced himself up onto all four paws, and quickly realized that he was in the bird's nest.

Get going! the voice in his head screamed.

The slightest movement made Henry wince in pain as he scrambled up and out of the nest. He found his footing on the branch where it was perched and crept along its length until he reached the trunk of the tree. By the time his paws touched down on solid ground he knew there was no time to waste. *Move! Now!* he commanded his body.

Henry ran as best as he could. The pain throbbed from nose to tail. He stopped often to catch his breath, unable to shake the feeling that he was being watched. He imagined the hawk's yellow eyes piercing into his back, but every time he checked behind him, he saw nothing.

Henry picked up the familiar scent of the field mice and followed it all the way to the stream that he'd seen them running toward from the sky. He reached the bridge and sniffed his way downstream. He lost the scent where the stream widened into a glassy, still pond. He stopped and held his ribs while he studied the terrain in front of him, then backtracked until he picked up the scent again and retraced his paw prints to the bridge. Standing on hind legs, he batted an ear and sniffed for clues, but the only thing he smelled was the stink on his own filthy fur.

Henry padded down to the water, splashed some on his belly and face, and sprayed some over his back. It hurt too much to shake dry, so he gently wiped the water from his fur. He was just smooth-ing his whiskers when he noticed a pair of ducks floating toward him in the middle of the pond. One of them had a green head with a bright white ring around its neck and breast feathers the color of chestnuts. When it turned and caught the sun's rays, the green feathers shimmered. *Like the queen's jewels,* Henry thought.

Henry sat on the grassy bank beneath the bridge and watched the ducks for a long time. Something about the way they glided together in such graceful silence across the shimmering water soothed his ragged nerves. *How can the world be filled with such beauty and such terror at the same time?* His eyelids grew heavy. He stretched out on his back and crossed one hind leg over another. Resting his head on clasped paws he told himself, *It's just for a minute.*

* * *

Henry woke with a jerk. Alarmed to discover that he had fallen asleep, he leaped up onto all fours and cocked his ears back and forth.

Just then Henry heard a splash. He turned, alert and ready to run if necessary. Rings rippled across the glassy water. A small fish broke through the surface and jumped into the air. The sun reflected off its silvery scales as it arched over backward into the water. Amazed and surprised, Henry hopped back, all the while keeping his eyes glued to the spot. He hoped to see the sparkly fish again, but it disappeared in the inky black pond.

"Did you see that?" came a voice, shattering the silence.

✦ 15 ✦
WISLEY

HENRY'S HEAD SNAPPED UP IN SURPRISE. His heart hammered in his chest as his eyes skimmed over the far shore . . . *a mouse!* Hope rose in his throat. *A field mouse!* He couldn't be sure if it was one from the group he'd seen before, but he waved a paw in the air and yelled, "Are you from around here? I'm lost." He hightailed it to the bridge to make his way across before the mouse ran away.

"Pretty close," hollered the mouse.

"Wait! I'm coming over," Henry shouted, moving as fast as his aching body would carry him.

When he got close enough, the mouse recognized Henry. His jaw dropped open and he pointed a paw. "You're Henry!" The sandy-brown mouse spoke first. He looked as if he had seen a ghost. "You're alive!"

Words caught in Henry's throat. He nodded. "Did you see where my friend went?"

"Jeremy? He's with us. He thinks you're . . ." The mouse paused. "Well, we *all* thought you were a goner." He shook his head in disbelief. "My name's Wisley, by the way." He extended a paw to Henry.

Relief rippled through every fiber of Henry's battered body as he shook paws with Wisley. He was so happy he could cry. "I can't believe it. I can't believe I found you," he sputtered as he straightened back up. Henry told Wisley how he'd seen the group from the sky, how he'd escaped from the nest and found his way here, hoping to catch up with them.

"I can't believe you got away," said Wisley. "Good thing I came out for my afternoon swim, or you might not have found *any* of us." Henry shook his head. He couldn't even think about it.

Henry smiled and swallowed hard. He wiped his cheeks with the back of his paws. He felt like hugging Wisley, but that might seem odd, so Henry held back.

"Are you badly hurt? Do you think you can follow me home? It's not too far from here."

"Just not too fast." Henry smiled weakly and waved Wisley on.

Checking over his shoulder often, Wisley guided Henry across the open field.

Paw over paw, they picked their way through the grasses. After what seemed like a long time, they reached a wooded grove.

"Almost there," Wisley squeaked reassuringly. "Boy, I bet you have a story that will curl our whiskers," he added, slowing.

Do I ever, thought Henry.

The entrance to Wisley's burrow was tucked between the roots of a large oak tree. Henry was just thinking that the hole looked painfully tight when Wisley said, "Don't worry. It widens as you go. The first chamber is my parent's nest, so pass that and go to the next one. I'll meet you there." And with that, Wisley plunged down the hole and was out of sight before Henry could shake a whisker.

⊹ 16 ⊹
NEVER GIVE UP

ONE BY ONE, EVERYONE REPORTED BACK
to Mother Mouse with bad news.

"Nobody's seen them!" they all said as they
gathered around the kitchen table midafternoon.
Mother Mouse excused herself and slipped away
down the hallway into Henry's room. She sat on
the edge of his bed and buried her face in her
paws.

The only other time Henry was gone this long,

without forewarning, was when Isabel went missing. She looked up at his decorated walls, remembering. A faint smile tugged at the corners of her mouth as Mother Mouse recalled how Henry and Jeremy had once rescued young Isabel by using a car from the dollhouse fleet. *He's resourceful,* she told herself. *Too cautious to get into trouble.* But a shadow of doubt danced up her spine. *It's a different world out there, though,* she fretted.

"What's the matter?" squeaked Isabel. "Are you thinking about Henry?"

"You scared me," said Mother Mouse when Isabel appeared at the entrance to Henry's bedroom. She could hardly look Isabel in the eye for fear that Isabel might be able to read her worst thoughts. Instead she looked down at a few tufts of bed fluff that needed smoothing.

Isabel wriggled onto Henry's bed beside Mother Mouse and dangled her petite hind paws over the edge. Mother Mouse wrapped a foreleg around Isabel and pulled her close. She rested her cheek on Izzy's head and closed her eyes.

While Mother Mouse snuggled with Isabel, her mind filled with thoughts of Henry. She studied the walls of his room, all covered with words from tour guides, wrappers, ticket stubs, and shopping lists. Her gaze stopped at the news clipping that hung above Henry's bed. It was from the local newspaper, the *Royal Rag*, and it told the story of the famous castle fire and her husband's heroic sacrifice to save others. Her heart ached all over again. She couldn't shake the thought of losing young Henry too.

She had to move. . . . *Do something! At least keep busy.* "Let's go make some crumb cakes," she said, nudging Isabel off the bed. "By the time they're done, I bet Henry will be home." She hoped she sounded convincing.

✱ ✱ ✱

By late afternoon, one cold crumb cake remained on the kitchen table. Mother Mouse paced frantically, trying not to look at the grim faces that still sat silent—waiting—hoping that Henry would come claim his cake. A soft whimper drew her attention back to them. Catching her eye, Alexander forced a smile while Isabel scowled at young Charlotte, whose mouth was quivering.

Mother Mouse stopped her pacing and wrung her paws. She opened her mouth to say something but closed it again. It was Isabel who broke the silence.

"Remember what Henry told me when I was locked in that trunk?" she said in her cheeriest voice. "'Never give up!' That's what he told me, so we *can't* give up on him!"

Mother Mouse felt her throat tighten as she watched her youngest try to raise their spirits.

"We can't give up on Henry. He didn't give up on me that time, and besides"—Isabel's eyes lit up—"think about the sticky situations he's been in and lived to twirl his tail." Isabel went on. "Like the time he got away from the fat rat that chased him through Rat Alley and the time he outsmarted Titus." Isabel slapped her small paw on the table. "And what about the car crash? If he could survive that, he can . . ." Her words trailed off and she clamped a paw to her mouth.

"You're so right!" Mother Mouse chimed in. "We can't think the worst. We can't give up hope!"

With a new sense of determination, Mother Mouse marched out of the kitchen. "Keep your ears open," she said over her shoulder. "I'm going upstairs." She didn't say exactly where.

SMALL WORLD

HENRY LANDED WITH A THUD IN THE bottom chamber of Wisley's dwelling. He felt dizzy with relief and faint from the pain. Wobbly and weak-kneed, he stood, instantly searching the burrow for Jeremy. A sea of mice—*Wisley's family*, Henry thought—crowded every nook and cranny.

"Henry!" shouted Jeremy, scrambling over to him.

"Still here." Henry smiled, shielding his ribs in case Jeremy was going to hug him.

Everyone started squeaking and chattering at once as they eyed the mouse they had heard so much about. Tails twitched with excitement while some waved their paws in the air and hurled questions at Henry.

"How did you get away?"

"Are you hurt?"

"He looks hurt."

"Where does it hurt?"

"How did you get here?"

"Give him a chance," Wisley shouted over the swarm of noses, whiskers, and ears huddled together. "Make way." He pushed a few back. "Give the poor guy room to breathe."

Henry smiled gratefully at Wisley and turned to face Jeremy. "It all happened so fast," Henry began. "One minute I was just nibbling a poppy seed and the next, I'm dangling from a claw, streaking through the sky."

There was stunned silence at first while all eyes were on Henry. As he told them about his close encounter with death, there were lots of *ooh*s and *aah*s and *oh no*s right up to his last sentence. "And then a voice out of nowhere said, 'Did you see that?' and that's when I found Wisley," Henry finished, waving the map to show Jeremy that he still had it.

Everyone chirped and cheered. Just then a husky voice boomed above the hubbub. "What's this all about?" The voice trailed off when he noticed the new face in the crowd.

Chatter dimmed to a low hum when a large mouse with a gray-brown hue, full whiskers, and a long, dark, bristly tail entered the chamber. He padded over toward Henry.

"Father, this is Henry Whiskers, the mouse we told you about . . . Jeremy's friend," said Wisley, hopping over to his father and waving a paw in Henry's direction.

"Name's Finnegan," said the older mouse to Henry.

Finnegan studied Henry from tip to tail and back again. Henry began to feel self-conscious. When he was finished, Finnegan humphed, as if he had made up his mind about something. He took two hops closer, squinted into Henry's eyes, and said, "It's remarkable! You look just like your father."

Henry opened his mouth to speak, but nothing came out.

"Did you know Henry's father?" Jeremy piped in, as if he were reading Henry's mind.

Finnegan wiggled his whiskers and grinned. "If it weren't for Henry's father, I probably wouldn't be here."

⇥ 18 ⇤
FELLOW TRAVELERS

"YOU ASKED IF I *'DID* KNOW' HENRY'S father. Has something happened to him?" asked Finnegan, searching Jeremy's and Henry's faces.

Jeremy saved Henry from having to explain. "Henry's father died in the big fire at Windsor Castle," Jeremy answered in hushed tones, "but not before rescuing Mrs. Myrtle Mouse and her children."

"You poor dear," said a round, short-whiskered

field mouse as she scampered over to them.

"I'm deeply saddened to hear that," said Finnegan.

"Me too," whispered Wisley.

An awkward silence followed. Henry turned away, and as he did he caught sight of a delicately whiskered golden mouse about his age. She held his gaze briefly and he felt heat rise in his cheeks.

"Finn, my love," the short-whiskered mouse squeaked, shifting Henry's attention back to the small group.

"Yes, my sweet," Finnegan replied in his deep voice.

Henry watched as Finnegan and his wife seemed to have a whole conversation without making a sound. By the end of it, Finnegan placed a paw on Henry's shoulder.

"This is my wife, Blossom, and my daughter over there is Fern," said Finnegan, tilting his head toward the mouse who had caught Henry's eye.

"It must have come as a shock to learn that I knew your father. We were fellow travelers," Finnegan said.

Henry's throat tightened like it always did when he thought about Father Mouse. A hundred questions raced through his mind. He didn't know where to begin, what to ask first, but it didn't matter. Finnegan explained.

"We met when we were young . . . not much older than you are now, I suppose." A warm smile peeked through Finnegan's silver-tipped whiskers. "We both wanted to see the world outside, beyond the walls of Windsor Castle."

"*You* lived in the castle?" Henry leaned in close.

Finnegan nodded. "In the Underground, just like Jeremy here." He pointed a paw at Jeremy. "Your father," he said, turning back to Henry, "read all those books in that library of yours. I think they inspired his sense of adventure . . . his desire to explore." Finnegan got a faraway look in his eyes as he recalled the story. "Your father inspired *me*, so I was determined to see the world for myself . . . smell it . . . taste it . . . feel the outdoor world under my own four paws."

Henry and Jeremy exchanged a knowing glance, as if they were hearing part of their own story.

One by one, Wisley's siblings slipped off to bed while Finnegan continued. "After several weeks, we ended up here in Windsor Great Park." He paused and took a deep breath. "I stayed," he sighed. "But your father didn't."

"Didn't he like country living?"

"He liked it very much. He even made that map you've got so he could find his way back."

Henry followed Finnegan's eyes to the map in his paw. "What happened? Why didn't he stay?"

"He had responsibilities," said Finnegan. "He

knew others counted on him to be the next care-
taker of the dollhouse."

"So I wasn't born yet?"

Finnegan shook his head. "I think he must have
met your mother after his travels."

Henry suddenly felt drained. Worn out and
overwhelmed, he tried to hide a yawn with his
paw while Finnegan leaned over the map and
started tapping the big ✘ with the tip of his tail.
Henry was just about to ask about the mysterious
mark when Blossom spoke up.

"You two must be knackered. I say it's time we
all got some sleep," she squeaked in a motherly
tone. "No more stories tonight." She clasped her
paws. "You sleep as long as you want," she added,
gently pinching each of them on a cheek.

"Good idea," Finnegan agreed. "You're going to
need all your strength if we're going to get you
home tomorrow."

"I like the sound of that," squeaked Jeremy.

"That makes two of us," Henry added.

"We'll make a plan at breakfast." Then Finnegan took Blossom by the elbow and led her to the tunnel up to their nest.

Wisley and Fern smiled good night. They turned toward the stacks of sleeping mice and tucked themselves in among their sisters and brothers. Henry and Jeremy found a patch of soft moss and collapsed. Henry closed his eyes and was just thinking that not even his sore ribs could keep him awake, when he felt Jeremy tap him on the back. "Hmm?"

"Do you get the feeling that Finnegan knows a lot more than he was telling us?" Jeremy whispered.

Yes! thought Henry as he felt himself drift into a deep, deep sleep.

✦ 19 ✦
CHANGE OF PLAN

TODAY'S THE DAY, THOUGHT HENRY AS HE and Jeremy arrived late to breakfast. They joined Wisley, Finnegan, and Fern around a mouth-watering selection of seeds, buds, berries, and sweet nectars, all neatly arranged across the top of a low-cut tree stump. As they crouched on a patch of sun-warmed pine needles, opposite the others, Henry felt as if Finnegan were an old friend. Since learning about his bond with

Father Mouse, Henry sensed that he could trust
Finnegan completely and was eager to plot a plan
for getting home.

At first they chattered back and forth about life
in Queen Mary's Dollhouse, Windsor Castle, and
outdoor survival in Windsor Great Park.

"Who knew that moss grows on the north side
of trees," squeaked Jeremy, stuffing a paw full of
wild clover into his mouth.

Everyone laughed except Finnegan, who seemed
lost in thought. *He hasn't said or eaten much of anything since we got here. What's up with him?* Henry
wondered. *I hope this doesn't have anything to do
with us.*

"Can we tell them about our idea now?" Wisley
asked enthusiastically.

With a nod from Finnegan, Wisley launched
in. "Fern and I had an idea." Wisley rubbed his
paws together and winked at Fern. "We thought

you might catch a ride home on the duke's carriage, so we sent some scouts out earlier to find out whether or not he took his morning ride."

Jeremy and Henry exchanged a confused look.

"What does that have to do with anything?" Jeremy asked.

Wisely smiled. "Let me explain. The duke usually drives his horse-drawn carriage into the park in the early morning or the late afternoon. One time of day or the other, but not both. It turns out that he didn't come this morning, so we are pretty positive that he'll come to watch the sunset late this afternoon. And when he does, he'll do what he always does and that will be your chance."

"What does he always do?" asked Henry.

"He'll stop at the top of the Long Walk, just below the statue of the Copper Horse, to get the best view of the castle."

"So that's when you jump onboard," squeaked Fern.

"And ride home in *styyyyle*," said Jeremy, pumping his paw in the air.

Henry shook his head. *How many times have I watched that carriage ride into the park?* he thought. *I never thought I'd get to ride on it one day.* "I love it!" He clapped his paws.

"All right then," said Wisley. "Let me show you on the map."

Jeremy flattened the map on the stump while Henry anchored its corners with acorns.

"We are right about here." Wisley stood on his hind legs and pointed to a spot on the map with his tail. "The Copper Horse and the Long Walk are there," he added.

"So close?" Henry couldn't believe it.

Wisley pointed a paw toward the top of a nearby hill.

"Whoa!" Jeremy's jaw dropped. "You mean that if we ran to the top of that hill and looked out over the other side, we would see the Long Walk and Windsor Castle?"

Henry sat silent, making sense of the plan. His eyes darted back and forth between the map, Jeremy, and the top of the hill that stood between them and home.

"But what happens if the duke *doesn't* come?"

Silence hung in the air just long enough to give Henry doubts.

"He'll come," said Finnegan. "He and the queen spend the month of Easter at Windsor Castle every year, but Easter Court is over after today, so they will be leaving tomorrow."

Henry let out a little puff of air. He liked the confidence in Finnegan's voice.

Fern piped up. "It's such a beautiful day. I'm sure he'll come to take one last ride."

"Could we just go back on paw if we had to?" asked Henry.

"Too risky," said Finnegan. "By day or night, the Long Walk is wide open to all kinds of trouble—people, dogs, deer, and *owls*! Besides, it's mowing season. Not good at all." He shook his head.

Henry was convinced when he heard the *O* word. *No more birds for me,* he thought.

"It's a good plan," Finnegan continued, clearing his throat and stroking his whiskers thoughtfully. Henry detected a *but* coming. "It's just the kind of thing your father would have done," Finnegan snuffed. "But there's something else you need to know." He hesitated again.

Henry held his breath again and leaned in to listen.

"It's my fault that I haven't mentioned it until now. I didn't know how . . ." Finnegan's words trailed off.

Henry glanced at Jeremy, who had flattened his ears and looked stiff as a stick.

"Your father left something with me that I think you should have," Finnegan burst out. "Problem is"—he cleared his throat again—"it's in our winter home back in the village."

Henry was dumbstruck. "What is it?" he half whispered.

"It's a book . . . well, maybe more like a diary." Finnegan bent over the map, planting his two front paws on either side of it. He traced the ragged edge of it and explained, "This was drawn on a page that was torn out of it." He paused. "Your father was teaching me to read before he left unexpectedly. I never knew what happened to him, but I'm glad to know he made it home and started a family." Finnegan raised his head and looked at Henry. His eyes twinkled as he continued. "I've only seen the pages, but I couldn't read them. The drawings and the words are written by paw, but I kept it safe all this time, hoping your father would return one day."

Henry swallowed hard. A memento that belonged to Father Mouse was more valuable than *all* the jewels in *all* the queen's crowns. "How far is the village?" Henry's voice quivered.

Finnegan pointed a paw toward the small village that sat on the far side of a nearby road and the fields beyond, dotted with sheep.

"So that's the big ✖ on the map?" Henry asked.

Finnegan nodded and smiled. "So your father could find his way back."

It all makes sense, thought Henry, staring at the map. In the quiet of the moment, he pictured his father tearing a page from the diary, drawing the map, and carefully marking the spot of greatest importance.

"There's not much time," Wisley warned.

Henry followed Wisley's eyes upward to the sky. The sun was straight overhead. "How long would it take to get there and back?"

Fern spoke up. "If you leave now, you might get back in time, but the duke doesn't stop for long. You'll have to be fast."

Finnegan chimed in. "Fern, you should be the one to take him. You know all the shortcuts." He cocked his head toward Wisley and said, "The two of us will take Jeremy to the Copper Horse statue and wait for you."

"Yes, Father," squeaked Fern. She flashed a smile at Henry.

Henry felt his heartbeat quicken—pumping through his paws as he readied himself for another race against time. Then something occurred to him. "Jeremy," he said, "if I don't make it back in time, you should go without me."

"No way!" squeaked Jeremy.

"He's right," said Finnegan, turning to Jeremy. "You could let his mother know that he's all right and that he has a place to stay until it's safe to return. Your family will be relieved to have you back. It's best for everyone, really."

It wasn't perfect, but nobody had any better ideas.

✦ 20 ✦
DETOUR

FERN WAS IN THE LEAD. SHE DASHED, darted, and lunged like an acrobat as they sprinted over leaves, out of the woods, across the road, and through furrowed fields on the far side. Henry raced to keep up. The distance between them grew as his bruised body slowed. When he finally caught up with her, she was watching for him, calmly nibbling on a blade of grass at the edge of a gully. At the bottom of the gully a thin stream of water trickled into a narrow pipe. Beyond the gully was another paved road, and beyond it stood a long row of houses that curved around a circle of green grass.

"Which house is yours?" puffed Henry, clasping his ribs.

"It's the General Store." Fern pointed her delicate paw at a red brick house with white trim and a picket fence in front. It faced the road. There was a large hedgerow to the right side of it, a garden with picnic tables on the left, and a sign on the fence that read BEWARE OF THE CAT. ENTER AT YOUR OWN RISK. Painted in gold letters over the front door and two large windows it said: WINDSOR GREAT PARK POST OFFICE AND GENERAL STORE. A red-and-gold crown was painted above that.

"Wow! This place looks cool." Henry smiled, but Fern was all business and didn't reply.

Fern eyed a green car as it passed by. "When the

coast is clear, we'll cross and follow that hedgerow just a little ways. There's a potted plant under the right front window and a gap in the brick siding right behind it. That's our entrance. It leads into the store." Fern pointed out the route. "Stay close," she warned.

"Do we have enough time?" he asked, still breathing hard. He tipped his head back to mark the sun. Their journey to this point had taken longer than he'd expected.

"We have to hurry," said Fern, as though she was thinking the same thing. She checked for cars. "Ready?"

Henry drew a deep breath and gave her the paws-up sign. Fern sprinted across the pavement. He stayed close on her paws. *Now is no time to lose sight of her,* he told himself.

When they reached the hedge, Fern slowed to a trot and paused where they had to cross over a terraced corner of ground and duck behind the potted plant. Just as she was about to launch, Henry blocked her. He pointed at a large black cat sprawled across the front doormat, sunning itself about twenty tail lengths beyond the flowerpot.

Fern slapped a paw over her mouth. "We've got no choice," she whispered. "There's no time."

Henry held his breath and followed her out of the hedge, behind the flowerpot, and into a crack in the brick.

They emerged inside between two large cardboard boxes marked *Walkers Ready Salted Potato Chips* and *Gourmet Cookies*. The only sound was a low hum that came from a large blue chest with pictures of popsicles and ice-cream cones on its side.

"Nobody's here," Fern whispered before she eased out onto a small patch of open floor. Henry followed, cautiously eyeing the human clutter that crowded the shop floor and dangled danger-ously over the countertops high above them. The air smelled of old newspapers, magazines, and clippings that curled at the corners and hung on the walls. It reminded Henry of his bedroom at home. His nose drew his attention to a counter display holding assorted candy bars, health bars, and sweet temptations. *If only there was time to explore,* he thought as Fern nudged him to keep moving.

They zigged and zagged between towering stacks of boxes, under the ice-cream chest, over a rotten floorboard, past the counters, and into a back room. Fern disappeared into a hole in the wall behind a large brown-and-orange checked armchair. Henry stayed close behind.

On the other side of the wall was a well-furnished nest for a large family of mice to live quite comfortably. There were several different nooks designed for different purposes. The largest, a family room, was padded with a fine layer of wood shavings while smaller spaces around its edges looked like they were lined with shredded tissues and colorful lengths of yarn. Here and there were personal collections and piles of soft pillow stuffing, dryer lint, and strips of fabric nibbled from human clothing.

Fern dove into a cranny filled with assorted paper clips, old wooden spools, and a rare shiny thimble. She sniffed frantically as Henry watched—helpless. "Ta-da!" she announced, pulling out a worn leather-bound book.

Henry hopped over to her. She smiled tenderly as she held it out to him. "I think this belongs to you," she whispered, placing it into his open paw.

It had a gold crown embossed on it, just like

the others he'd seen in the dollhouse library. Henry's heart skipped. He couldn't resist fanning through its pages. At a quick glance he saw paw prints and scratchy writing. "I think your father's right," Henry muttered. "Definitely a diary of some kind."

"We better go," Fern squeaked sympathetically. "You can read it when you get home."

Henry's heart tugged in his chest. He forced himself to shut the book. Its hidden secrets would have to wait.

With the diary firmly lassoed in his tail, Henry gave Fern the paws-up sign and in no time they were back outside, peeking out from behind the flowerpot.

When Henry didn't see the dog on the door-mat, he remembered a famous joke among mice. *It's never a good sign when the pet's not where you left it.* "Psst." He wanted to warn Fern, but it was too late. She was off and running toward the hedge.

Afraid of getting separated, he held his breath and darted after her. That's when he saw a streak of something black and very large from the corner of his eye.

✦ 21 ✦
NO CHOICE

"FASTER!" HENRY HOLLERED AFTER FERN.

She glanced back at him. Her frightened expression told him all he needed to know. He could feel the cat close behind as he dove into the hedge. Its enormous paw jabbed in after him, barely missing its mark. The diary caught on a low branch. Henry tugged it loose and swiftly switched it from tail to paw. With it clutched tightly to his chest he continued, darting left and right through the thick tangle of branches. *Just get to the pipe,* Henry told himself. *The cat can't fit in there!*

At the end of the hedge Henry saw Fern stopped on the far side of the road, looking back—her eyes sweeping back and forth, searching for him. He leaped into the road. Desperate to reach the other side and the safety of the ground pipe, he was focused only on Fern. When he saw her black eyes widen and her mouth open to call out, a deafening roar brought him to his senses. He turned and saw a bright red truck heading straight for him.

Think! Fast! Henry looked back behind him. *Cat! No way.* He judged the distance to Fern. His heart pounded in his ears as his legs crouched, ready to spring. *One... two... oops... NOW!*

Henry power-punched his hind legs and hurled himself into the air, feeling the weight of the book. He barely sprang clear of the tires as they whizzed past. He somersaulted through the air and landed hard on his bruised side while a cloud of dirt and gravel rained down on him. Still clutching the diary, he rolled down into the gully.

"Get up!" Fern ordered, helping yank him to his paws. "He's coming."

Over her head, Henry spied the cat. Somehow Henry managed to stumble into the pipe and out of reach just in time. _Whoosh,_ went the black paw, just missing Henry's tail. _Hiss,_ came its foul breath. Henry and Fern tumbled backward—further out of reach—and caught their breath.

"That was too close," Fern trembled. "You scared me to death."

"Me too," gasped Henry.

Henry followed Fern's gaze as she stared down the length of the pipe that disappeared into pitch-black darkness. "Where does this go?" he asked. She turned to face him and shrugged her shoulders.

"Not sure," she said, "but we have no choice." She pointed a paw toward the cat that was patrolling by the near end of the ground pipe. "I just hope it will lead us where we want to go in time."

✦ 22 ✦
READY, SET, GO

IT FELT LIKE *FOREVER* BEFORE THEY caught a glimpse of daylight. When they finally reached the other end of the pipe, the two of them stopped in the stripy shadows coming from the grate overhead. Henry peered up. His heart sank when he noticed the rosy hue of a single cloud floating across the sky.

"Don't give up!" squeaked Fern, as if she could sense Henry's concern.

She's right, he thought. Just then he had an idea. "Hold this!" He handed her the diary. "Think you can reach the grate if I give you a boost?"

Fern smiled, obviously game to try.

Henry bent over and cupped his front paws together. "Ready?"

Fern stepped up with her hind paw and leaned a front paw on his back for balance.

"Set?" He felt her straighten.

"Go!" she shouted.

Henry propelled her upward. She was light as a feather and practically flew through the iron slats of the grate.

"Hang on. I'll be right back," she hollered down from the ground above.

Do I have a choice? Henry wondered as he paced back and forth. *Breathe in . . . breathe out . . . slowwwwwlyyyyyy.* He tried to calm himself.

"Watch out below!" Fern yelled after several

long minutes. She lowered a long, smooth vine through the grate. It made a small splash when it hit bottom.

Henry's heart leaped. *Brilliant!* He wrapped all four paws around it and scrambled up as fast as he could. Fern lent him a paw at the top as he wriggled through the grate and gained his footing. But when he noticed where they were and the long shadows that spread across the road in front of them, Henry let out a heavy sigh. They were farther down the road than they wanted to be—far from the hill with the Copper Horse, and the late-day light told him that the sun was nearly setting. His shoulders slumped. He kicked the ground and tsked. "Where are we?" He could practically taste his disappointment as his throat tightened and he struggled to hold back tears.

Just then his thoughts were interrupted by a sound coming from up the road.

Fern heard it too. "We're farther than we should be ..." Her words trailed off as she spun to face the sound. Her ears perked as she stared up the road. "But we might still have a ..." She stopped. She stared, openmouthed and wide-eyed.

Henry followed her gaze.

From around a bend came four dark horses trotting in pairs, one pair in front of the other, pulling a carriage behind them.

"Is that?" The words stuck in his throat. "It looks like ..." He glanced back at Fern and searched her face for clues. She smiled at the same time that she shook her golden-brown head from side to side in disbelief.

"Your chariot has arrived," Fern said, waving a graceful paw toward the duke's carriage as it trotted toward them. "It's not too late after all. "

This is it! I'm going home! Joy, relief, fear, and sorrow swept over him.

But…suddenly, Henry wasn't ready to leave. He looked at Fern. Everything was happening too fast.

Clop-clop-clop. The horses were fast approaching.

"The book," Fern said, thrusting it into Henry's paws.

Henry looked down at the book and remembered. He *had to* go home. Like Father Mouse before him, Henry held a special place in his family. He was needed … he was loved … and he loved them too.

Clop-clop-clop.

Henry's eyes darted up the road then back to Fern's. "Thank you," he whispered with a heavy heart. His thoughts scrambled together as so many feelings swirled inside him and he searched for words to express them.

Clop-clop-clop.

No time, thought Henry, and just as he leaned in to give Fern a hug, she did the same.

"It's coming!" she squeaked, pulling away and nudging him to take his position.

Henry took one last longing look at Fern, then spun on his tail and hopped out into the road—not so far to be squished. His heart banged in his chest as he hopped closer to the spot where he hoped he could make the jump without getting trampled. He curled his tail tight around the book and freed his paws. He fixed his eyes on the carriage. Nothing else mattered now as he calculated.

The ground quaked under Henry's paws as sixteen horse hooves pounded toward him. The black spokes on the wheels pin-wheeled and blurred . . . closer . . . closer. *Gotta be fast.* As the rig approached, Henry pointed himself in the same direction that the carriage was traveling and started to run.

Clippety-clippety-clippety-clop!

The little voice in Henry's head took over, guiding his every move.

Run! Get behind ... see the step ... JUMP!

His hind legs burned with the thrust as his front paws found their perch and held tight while he hoisted himself up onto the rear carriage step. The moment he felt secure, seated on the hard metal spot, Henry searched the distance where he had just stood with Fern. She was already gone.

✦ 23 ✦
LAST STOP

HENRY WEDGED THE BOOK INTO A CRACK between the rear step and the carriage frame. He clung tight with his tail and watched as the grove of trees, the fields, the village, and the places he had just come to know all disappeared in the distance. His heart ached and he wondered, *How can I feel so happy and so sad all at once?*

The carriage suddenly swayed sideways as it rounded a bend in the road. Henry pressed his paws down on either side of him for balance and closed his eyes. When he felt the carriage straighten and begin to slow, he opened them again. With the woods behind them, the wide-open sky above was painted purply blue, and to the west it dissolved into shades of scarlet, pink, and orange. On the downhill side of the carriage, the slope of the hill flattened into grassland dotted with deer out for their evening graze. Henry knew where he was now. He'd seen it a hundred times from behind the castle windows. His heart thumped harder in anticipation.

Sure enough, the carriage slowed to a crawl, turned, and stopped, *just like they said it would.* Henry was facing the Copper Horse statue while the duke, seated at the front of the carriage, looked down the length of the Long Walk toward Windsor Castle at the far end, sitting in the glow of the setting sun.

"Jeremy!" Henry yelled as his best friend sprinted out from under a rock and bounded across the road toward the carriage. Henry saw Finnegan and Wisley standing by the rock, waving their paws in the air.

Henry cheered as Jeremy hurtled himself through the air onto the black shiny spokes of the carriage wheel. "Grab on," yelled Henry, extending his tail when Jeremy reached the top rim and was ready to make the leap onto the step next to him.

"Whew!" Jeremy panted. "You had me worried. Did you get the diary? Can I see it?"

Henry shook his head. "Too bouncy," he said. Then he warned, "Hang on. Use your tail, like this."

Henry curled his tail around the lip of the step, removed the book from where it was wedged, and then quickly sat on it.

The carriage lurched forward with a massive jerk and began to roll down the slope of the hill toward home. Henry and Jeremy exchanged a look and high-pawed each other. As they picked up speed, Henry glanced back to the rise of the road and the Copper Horse above it. *It will never look the same again,* he thought as he imagined the view from back at the castle. Just then, before it was too late, he spied three small silhouettes of his new friends. *I'll be back!* Henry silently promised as he and Jeremy continued on their long way home.

⊹ 24 ⊹
AT LONG LAST

MOTHER MOUSE HID BEHIND A GRATE IN the upstairs wall of the castle and waited for the right moment.

"Five o'clock," Warden hollered to the castle visitors. "Closing time. Please exit to your right."

It was the same thing every evening. There were always a few humans who straggled, as if they were deaf to Warden's instructions. *Soon enough,* she told herself. *Be patient.*

By the time Warden escorted the last of the visitors out of the castle and went home for the day, Mother Mouse could hardly wait a second longer. She anxiously leaped onto the nubby red carpet, scurried along its edge to the window that had the best view, and hopped up onto its golden oak sill. From there she took a long, slow sniff and tried to calm herself.

"The world is full of mysteries." That's what her husband had told her the day he brought her to that very spot and showed her the map he'd made. "I will take you there one day," he promised, waving the map toward the world beyond the glass. She could practically feel him standing beside her, nuzzling close.

A whimper escaped from her as she wiped her tears from her cheek.

Her instinct told her that Henry was out there, on the other side of the glass . . . beyond the safety of home. It was the only explanation that made sense, given all the clues. Her throat tightened, and she felt as if she couldn't breathe. She gasped for air and leaned a paw against the cool glass to steady herself.

From where she stood, Mother Mouse had a perfect view of the Copper Horse at the far end of the Long Walk. The waning sun cast its last rosy rays onto the statue and the duke's carriage, which was making its way back home. Her teary eyes followed the horse-drawn carriage as it slid down the distant hill and drew closer. By the time it glided through the castle's gold-tipped gates, all but the last light of day had disappeared.

Another day gone by and no Henry. A tear slipped from a whisker as she forced herself up to go home. But outside, the gravelly sound of horse hooves in the courtyard drew her attention. Her ears pricked up and she glanced out the window one last time. The carriage stopped directly below. Her heart leaped when she caught sight of two small figures streaking across the gravel and disappearing into the castle. *Could it be? It has to be. Who else . . . ?*

So many thoughts rushed at her all at once. Mother Mouse didn't hesitate. She flew off the sill and onto the floor. She hardly knew where she was heading. She raced as fast as her legs would carry her to see for herself—to be certain she hadn't imagined it.

And while Mother Mouse was closing the distance between them, Henry waved Jeremy goodbye where their paths parted.

Jeremy hesitated. "What are you going to do with that?" he asked, cocking his head toward the diary in Henry's paw.

Henry had been wondering the same thing. Finally home now, every whisker wilted with the weight of exhaustion, and yet his heart still raced from the thrill of it all.

Jeremy pointed a paw at Henry's prize, prompting an answer.

Who knew what tales it might tell . . . what secrets it might reveal. "Promise you won't tell?" Henry whispered.

Jeremy nodded at once.

"I think I'll keep it to myself," Henry hesitated. "To read before everyone else gets their paws on it." There! He'd decided—not without a hint of guilt—but certain, for the moment, that it was the right thing to do.

A silent agreement passed between the two as they high-pawed each other and turned for home.

QUEEN MARY'S DOLLHOUSE, where Henry lives, is a real dollhouse that is located in Windsor Castle in Windsor, England. For more information about it, please visit:

https://www.royalcollection.org.uk/visit/windsorcastle/what-to-see-and-do/queen-marys-dolls-house

The house being packed up in the Mansfield Street drawing room, where its architect, Sir Edwin Lutyens, lived.